OLD TOM

HARRIS.
LION POWER

abc7
ABC 7 CHICAGO

HYPERION
BOOKS FOR CHILDREN

RADIO Disney
AM 1300

This Book Awarded To: _____

For participating in The Power to Read

Look out for these Old Tom books . . .

Old Tom Goes to Mars
Old Tom's Guide to Being Good
Old Tom Goes to the Beach

LEIGH HOBBS

HYPERION PAPERBACKS FOR CHILDREN

New York

Copyright © 1994 by Leigh Hobbs

All rights reserved. No part of this book may be reproduced or transmitted in any form or by any means, electronic or mechanical, including photocopying, recording, or by any information storage and retrieval system, without written permission from the publisher. For information address Hyperion Books for Children, 114 Fifth Avenue, New York, New York 10011-5690.

First U.S. paperback edition, 2005

10 9 8 7 6 5 4 3 2 1

Printed in the United States of America

Library of Congress Cataloging-in-Publication Data on file.

ISBN 0-7868-5513-4

Visit www.hyperionbooksforchildren.com

For Ann James and Jenny Melican

Angela Throgmorton lived alone and liked
it that way. One day, while doing some light
dusting, she heard a knock at the door.

There, on her front step, was a baby monster.

Angela was curious, so she carried him in . . .

And brought him up.

Angela had never fed a baby before,
and what a strange big baby he was!
She called him "Old Tom."

Old Tom grew up very quickly. In fact, it
wasn't long before he outgrew his playpen.

And when he did, Angela gave him the spare
room. It was all clean and neat.

Angela taught Old Tom how to behave.
"Sit up straight!" she would say.
"Elbows off the table."

"Not too much on your fork."
"Chew with your mouth closed."

There was so much to learn.

But Old Tom loved bath time most of all,
when he could splash about and make a mess.

He always liked to look his best . . .

especially when he went out to play.

At first, Angela ignored Old Tom's childish pranks.

After all, she had things to do and
dishes to wash.

But her heart sank when *someone*
forgot his manners.

Old Tom *tried* to be good . . .

though sometimes he was a bit naughty.

"Aren't you a little too old for such things?"
Angela Throgmorton often asked.

As the months went by, Angela tried to
keep the house tidy.

It wasn't easy, as Old Tom seemed
to be everywhere.

There was no doubt about it,

he was a master of disguise.

Sometimes Angela heard strange noises
coming from the kitchen,

and whenever she had guests, Old Tom
would drop in unannounced.

Old Tom was out of control.

"When *will* you grow up?" Angela often muttered under her breath.

Sometimes Old Tom went for a little walk
to the mailbox.

But Angela thought it best that he stay
inside. "You mustn't frighten the neighbors,"
she would say.

When babies came to visit . . .

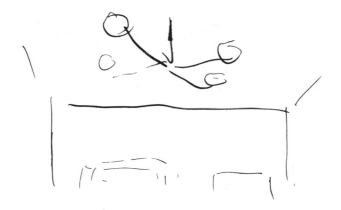

Old Tom loved to play.

"Heavens, what is that in the carriage with
my baby!" cried one of Angela's friends during
afternoon tea one day.

It was Old Tom, of course.
Angela was extremely embarrassed.

By now, Angela was having trouble sleeping.

Her nerves were shattered.

And Old Tom's fur had given her
dreadful hay fever.

When she finally did fall
asleep, Old Tom was
often in her dreams.

Angela longed for the good old days,
when her home was in order . . .

with everything in its place.

Whenever it was time to help with the dishes,
Old Tom felt sick.

He liked to sleep in, and enjoy a late breakfast
in Angela's favorite armchair.

Angela was fed up.

Old Tom had to go.

"At last I have the house to myself!"
cried Angela Throgmorton.

It was a bold move,

but Angela thought it was for the best.

Now she was free to scrub . . .
and polish,
sweep, and mop.

With Old Tom gone, her house would be spick-and-span once more.

But now Old Tom was in town,

where there were places to see
and people to meet.

In the pet shop nearby, he found new friends to play with.

Some had feathers and one had fins.

But Fluffy the puppy was
Old Tom's favorite.

In the cinema next door, the film had just started.

When Old Tom wandered in . . .

he was mistaken for a monster on the screen.

It was a wonderful surprise when
Old Tom found Happyland.

There were swings and slides,

places to hide,

children to play with . . .

and an elephant to ride.

Old Tom was having a lovely time.

But not everyone was happy in Happyland.

When darkness fell, Old Tom was alone.

And when the storm came, he tried
to be brave,

even when the thunder boomed.

For Old Tom there was
no breakfast or lunch,

or afternoon tea . . .

While far away, Angela was alone in her clean, tidy home.

Old Tom tried to find someone to play with.

But he couldn't find one friendly face.

There was no fur on her floor, but Angela
still couldn't sleep.

And neither could Old Tom.

He had nowhere to
go and nothing to eat,

until at last he found food at the
bottom of a trash can,

where he dreamed of his warm, safe bed.

Angela was worried sick.

For poor Old Tom . . .

the future looked bleak.

Suddenly, there was a news flash:
"ORANGE FURRY MONSTER CAUGHT."

"That monster is my baby!" cried
Angela Throgmorton.

In no time at all, she was off to the
pound to rescue Old Tom.

"Be quick!" Angela shrieked.

Inside the cage,
Old Tom had just begun to cry,

when suddenly, he heard a big voice boom:
"I'm here for my baby!"

Angela was overjoyed.

And so was Old Tom.

ABOUT THE AUTHOR

Leigh HOBBS

was born in Melbourne in 1953, but grew up in a country town called Bairnsdale. Leigh wrote and illustrated *Horrible Harriet*, which was shortlisted for the 2002 Children's Book Council of Australia Book of the Year Awards, in addition to the Old Tom books (*Old Tom, Old Tom Goes to Mars, Old Tom Goes to the Beach*, and *Old Tom's Guide to Being Good*). Leigh has two dogs, a blue heeler and a kelpie. He feels no affinity with cats, with one notable exception.

Join **OLD TOM**
on his next adventure!

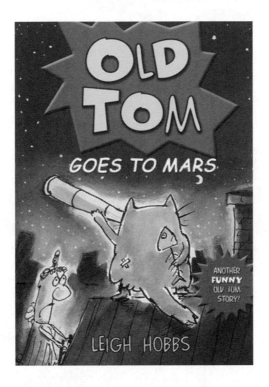